This
Book Belongs to

_____

Read all about your favorite bear!

Walt Disney's
The Many Adventures of
Winnie the Pooh

A Classic Disney Treasury

Disney
PRESS

NEW YORK

Contents

Introduction

The stories about Winnie the Pooh and his friends in the Hundred-Acre Wood are beloved classics, translated into dozens of languages and adored by children everywhere. For them, he's the lovable, huggable friend who shares their innocence and endless curiosity. For adults, Pooh represents the most admirable traits of childhood: a perception of a world filled with simplicity and beauty, and the security of steadfast friendship.

Walt Disney and everyone's favorite bear at Disneyland, circa 1965

The story of Winnie the Pooh began when A. A. Milne's son, Christopher Robin, received the gift of a stuffed bear on his first birthday. "Edward Bear" was renamed Winnie the Pooh after "Winnipeg," a Canadian black bear at the London Zoo, and a swan Christopher Robin had named "Pooh." Mr. Milne was a successful author and playwright, and the friendship between Christopher Robin and Pooh-bear became an inspiration.

Winnie the Pooh's adventures began as bedtime stories told to Christopher Robin by his father, but soon they were being read to boys and girls everywhere. Milne published *Winnie the Pooh* in 1926, with accompanying illustrations by English artist Ernest H. Shepard.

Winnie the Pooh was followed by *The House at Pooh Corner* in 1927.

A continent away, and decades later, Walt Disney was one of thousands of parents who shared these stories with his children. Inspired by his children's love for Pooh, Walt acquired the rights to several stories in 1961 and started plans for a musical animated feature-length film. Later, Walt changed his plans and decided to release three "featurettes," each one with a Milne classic tale at its heart.

Disney veteran Wolfgang Weitherman was brought on board as the producer and director, and the talented songwriting team of Richard M. and Robert B. Sherman, renowned for their work on *Mary Poppins,* were asked to capture the spirit of Milne's work. Buddy Baker wrote, arranged, and conducted the musical score to complement the songs written by the Sherman brothers.

Animator Norma Swank hand-inking Christopher Robin

Walt realized the value of staying consistent with his audience's childhood memories of these tales and insisted that his artists adhere as much as possible to the original characters as conceived by Ernest Shepard in his charming illustrations. When the designs of the characters were approved, model sheets were created so each animator had a reference for how the characters were to be drawn. The overall art design for the film kept the feel of Shepard's line-drawn backgrounds as well. In the end, over thirty artists worked to create these animated classics.

Once the story and the characters were approved, but before the animation could begin, the dialogue had to be recorded. Casting the voices for this stuffed menagerie brought out many of Hollywood's most interesting talents.

Actor Sterling Holloway, the voice of the Cheshire Cat in *Alice in Wonderland*, was cast as Winnie the Pooh. Character actor John Fiedler provided the voice of timid Piglet; Paul Winchell provided the voice of the irrepressible Tigger; and Sebastian Cabot, best known as Mr. French of *A Family Affair*, narrated Pooh's adventures.

On February 4, 1966, *Winnie the Pooh and the Honey Tree* was released theatrically. Shortly after *The Honey Tree* was released, Walt started production on the second featurette, the Academy-Award-winning *Winnie the Pooh and the Blustery Day*, released in 1968 after Walt Disney's death. In keeping with Walt's original intentions, the Disney Studios created *Winnie the Pooh and Tigger Too* and

Sterling Holloway (left) and Sebastian Cabot (right) create the magic of Pooh.

released it in 1974. In 1977, all three were combined in the full-length feature *The Many Adventures of Winnie the Pooh*. There was still one tale that had yet to be made into an animated classic, and in 1983 *Winnie the Pooh and a Day for Eeyore* was released.

Today, Walt Disney's Winnie the Pooh is an intrinsic part of childhood the world over.

WALT DISNEY'S

Winnie the Pooh
and the Honey Tree

Janet Campbell

Illustrated by John Kurtz

In a little house deep in the Hundred-Acre Wood, a very round bear named Winnie the Pooh was doing his slimming exercises. He was breathing deeply when, all of a sudden, he felt his tummy rumble.

"Oh my," said Pooh. "This up-and-downing is making me hungry."

Pooh hurried to the cupboard and got out his honeypot.

"Bother!" said Pooh. "There's nothing left but the sticky part."

But the sticky part was better than *no* honey at all so Pooh stuck his nose into the pot and licked up the last little bit.

With his head deep inside the pot, Pooh heard a buzzing sound. "That buzzing means something," Pooh said.

Pop! He pulled his head out and saw a bee fly out his window.

"Buzzing means bees," said Pooh. "And where there are bees, there's usually honey!"

Pooh followed the bee through the Hundred-Acre
Wood. When he came to the foot of a very tall tree, he
looked up and saw the bee buzzing around a hole.

"Honey!" said Pooh, and he began to climb. He climbed
and he climbed, all the way up the tree, all the way up to
the hole.

As Pooh leaned forward, the branch began to bend. The more he leaned, the more the branch bent, until he could *almost* reach the honey.

He leaned just a little bit more and . . . *snap!* went the branch and down fell Pooh.

He bounced from branch . . . to branch . . . to branch . . .

until he ran out of branches . . .

and landed headfirst in a bush!

"Oh my," said Pooh, rubbing his sore head. "I guess it all comes from liking honey so much!"

Pooh rubbed his head so hard that he came up with an idea—he would borrow a balloon from his friend Christopher Robin!

"You can't get honey with a balloon," Christopher Robin told Pooh.

"*I* can," said Pooh. "I shall hang on to the string and float up to the bee hole," he explained.

Then Pooh rolled himself in mud until he was covered from his nose to his toes.

"I'm pretending to be a little black storm cloud," Pooh told Christopher Robin, "to fool the bees."

"Silly old bear," said Christopher Robin. He watched Pooh float up, up, up into the sky and dangle right beside the hole.

Pooh reached in and pulled out a pawful of golden honey as the bees began to buzz suspiciously around his head.

"Christopher Robin!" called Pooh. "I think the bees suspect that I am not a little black storm cloud!"

With a swoosh, the balloon's string loosened and the balloon began to lose air. It swooshed under Pooh and it swooshed over Pooh, and then it rose high above the treetops, with Pooh trailing along for the ride.

"Oh my," said Pooh.

Then the balloon had no more air at all, and down Pooh went, landing right on top of Christopher Robin!

"Oh dear," said Pooh, shaking his head. "I guess it all comes from liking honey so much!"

By then it was lunchtime, and Pooh was hungrier than ever. So he sat down to think, and he thought first about honey and then about Rabbit, because Rabbit always had some honey in his house.

Pooh hurried to Rabbit's house.

"Uh . . . er . . . come in, Pooh," said Rabbit.

"Why, thank you, Rabbit," said Pooh.

"How about some lunch?" Rabbit asked, knowing perfectly well

what Pooh's answer would be. "Would you like condensed milk or honey on your bread?"

"Both," Pooh answered. "But never mind the bread," he added so as not to appear greedy.

Rabbit sat at the table and watched Pooh eat.

First, Pooh had a little helping of condensed milk and then a little helping of honey. Then he had another helping of condensed milk and another helping of honey. Pooh ate and ate and ate and ate.

At last, Pooh rose slowly from the table and said in a rather
sticky voice, "Good-bye, Rabbit, I must be going."

Rabbit sighed. "Well, Pooh, if you're sure you won't have any
more . . ."

"*Is* there any more?" asked Pooh.

"No," said Rabbit wearily, "there isn't."

"I thought not," said Pooh, and he started out Rabbit's front
door.

Pooh's head reached the outdoors and his feet dangled indoors, but his middle got stuck in the middle! Pooh tried to go out. He couldn't. He tried to go in. But he couldn't do that either.

"Bother!" said Pooh. "It all comes from not having a big enough front door."

"Nonsense!" said Rabbit sharply. "It all comes from eating too much!" And he hurried out his back door to fetch Christopher Robin.

Now there was nothing for Pooh to do but wait. He looked at the trees blowing in the breeze. He watched the clouds sailing by in the blue sky. Then he wiggled his bottom and kicked his legs — just in case — but he was still stuck tight.

So he looked at the trees some more and spotted Owl sitting on a branch.

"Hello, Pooh," said Owl. "Are you stuck?"

"Oh, no!" said Pooh. "I'm just resting."

Owl swooped down from his branch. "Pooh," he said, "you are definitely stuck. You are a wedged bear in a great tightness. This situation calls for an expert!"

"Did someone say 'expert'?" asked Gopher. "Gopher's my name, digging's my game. Now, what seems to be the problem?"

He quickly inspected the situation. "The problem with this door," Gopher said, "is that it has a bear in it. Now we could dig him out, or we could dynamite him out."

"Dynamite?" Pooh said in a very small voice.

"Dynamite!" exclaimed Owl. "Nonsense! We can't dynamite. We might hurt him!"

"Well, think it over," said Gopher, popping back down into his hole. "Let me know if you change your mind."

Finally Rabbit returned with Christopher Robin close behind.

"Silly old bear," said Christopher Robin, shaking his head. Then he took hold of Pooh's paw, and Rabbit took hold of Christopher Robin's shirt, and they pulled and pulled and pulled.

But Pooh was still stuck tight.

"Pooh Bear," said Christopher Robin, "there is only one thing to do. We will just have to wait for you to get thin!"

So they all waited.
Christopher Robin
read stories to Pooh.

Owl lectured him on the
dangers of eating too much.

Kanga brought Pooh a kerchief
to protect his head from the sun.

Eeyore made gloomy
predictions about how long
it might take for Pooh to get
thinner. "It could be days,"
he said with a sigh. "Maybe
weeks, even months," he
added.

Rabbit grew tired of seeing Pooh's bottom and legs where his front door used to be, so he wedged a picture frame around Pooh and put a lace doily on Pooh's bottom. "And now for a little dash of color," he said, and set a flowerpot on top of the doily on top of Pooh. But Pooh kicked his legs and the flowerpot went crashing to the ground.

Next, Rabbit found two branches that looked like antlers. With a paintbrush, he painted a moose face right on Pooh's bottom.

For a finishing touch, Rabbit found a board and put it across Pooh's legs like a shelf. "Now that's more like it!" he said.

More time passed, and still Pooh wasn't getting any thinner.

Kanga brought Roo for a visit. "I brought you some honeysuckle, Pooh," said Roo.

"*Honey*suckle?" asked Pooh hungrily.

"No, Pooh," said Kanga, laughing. "You don't eat it—you smell it."

Pooh buried his nose in the flowers and sniffed.

"Mmmmm," he said. He sniffed again. "Ahhhh." Then his nose began to tickle. "Ahhhh," he said once more. "Ah, ah, ah . . . . . . *choo*!"

Down came Rabbit's new shelf, knickknacks and all.

"Oh dear! Oh dear!" said Rabbit crossly. "Why did I ever invite that bear to lunch?"

That night, Pooh was awakened by Gopher, who popped up to eat his midnight lunch.

Pooh watched hungrily as Gopher ate. When Gopher took a honeypot from his lunch box, Pooh just couldn't stand it any longer. "Please, Gopher," he pleaded, "could you spare a small smackeral of honey?"

Inside, Rabbit heard voices. Why, he was sure he had just heard someone give Pooh some honey—honey that would make him fatter and keep him stuck in Rabbit's front door even longer!

"Stop, stop, stop!" Rabbit cried, and he rushed out his back
door and around to the front just in time to snatch a honeypot from
Pooh's paws. "Not a bite!" he snapped. "Not a lick! Not a drop!"

Then he made a sign and stuck it right up in front of Pooh where everyone could see it.

The next morning, Rabbit was busy tidying up. He mopped his brow and leaned against Pooh's bottom to rest.

Pooh moved!

"He budged! Hooray! He budged!" Rabbit cried. "He bidged! He badged! He boodged!"

He stopped to catch his breath. "Christopher Robin!" he said. "I must get Christopher Robin!"

And out his back door Rabbit went, off through the Hundred-Acre Wood, just as fast as he could go.

Before Pooh knew it, along came a parade of his very good friends.

Rabbit ran into his house and began to push Pooh's bottom.

Christopher Robin grabbed Pooh's paws. Kanga grabbed Christopher Robin, Eeyore grabbed Kanga, Roo grabbed Eeyore, and they all pulled as hard as they possibly could.

Just when they were beginning to think that perhaps Pooh hadn't budged after all, Rabbit backed up in his living room as far as he could go and ran across the floor as fast as he could run and threw himself at Pooh's bottom as hard as he could throw himself.

Pop!

Pooh flew out the doorway like a cork from a bottle and sailed across the grassy place in front of Rabbit's house—straight toward another honey tree. He landed headfirst right inside the hole in the tree.

Buzzzzz! Pooh's sudden appearance startled the bees, and they
flew out of the tree and far away over the treetops.

Winnie the Pooh considered his new surroundings. Everywhere he looked, he saw delicious, delightful, mouth-watering honey.

"Don't worry, Pooh!" called Christopher Robin from way down below. "We'll get you out!"

"Take your time, Christopher Robin," said Pooh. "Take your time!"

Walt Disney's

Winnie the Pooh
and the Blustery Day

Teddy Slater

Illustrated by Bill Langley and Diana Wakeman

One fine day, the East Wind traded places with the West Wind, and that stirred things up a bit in the Hundred-Acre Wood.

And on that windy day, Winnie the Pooh decided to visit his Thoughtful Spot. As he walked along, he made up a little hum. This is how it went:

Oh, the wind is lashing lustily,

and the trees are thrashing thrustily,

and the leaves are rustling gustily,

so it feels that it will undoubtedly be . . .

a rather blustery day!

As soon as Pooh reached his Thoughtful Spot, he sat right down and tried to think of something.

"Think, think, think, think, think," Pooh mumbled to himself. But nothing came to mind.

"Think, think, think," Pooh tried again, putting one paw to his head as if to catch any stray thoughts that might come wandering along.

Suddenly Gopher popped out of his gopher hole and said, "What's wrong, sonny? Got yourself a headache?"

"No," Pooh replied. "I was just thinking."

"Is that so?" said Gopher. "Well, if I were you, I'd think about skedaddling out of here. It's Windsday, you know."

"Windsday? Why, so it is," said Pooh. And then he finally had a thought—and it was a good one, at that. "I think I shall go wish everyone a happy Windsday," Pooh announced. "And I shall begin with my very dear friend Piglet."

Piglet lived in the middle of the forest in a very grand house. And on this blustery day, he was sweeping the fallen leaves away from his front door. He had just swept the last leaf away when a big gust of wind blew it right back at him, scooping him up and whisking him away. "I don't mind the leaves that are leaving . . . ," Piglet observed. "It's the leaves that are coming." And with that, he was blown right into Pooh Bear.

"Happy Windsday," said Pooh as another great gust of wind lifted Piglet right off his little pink feet.

"Well, it isn't very happy for me," Piglet said with a gulp.

"Where are you going?" Pooh cried, running after his friend.

"That's what I'm asking myself," Piglet said. "Where . . . ?"

"And what do you think you will answer yourself?" Pooh asked, grabbing hold of Piglet's scarf just before he floated out of reach.

"Oh, Pooh, I'm unraveling!" Piglet cried.

Indeed he was. Or rather, his scarf was. Like a pink kite on a long green string, Piglet went sailing off into the sky.

"Oh dear. Oh d-d-d-dear, dear," he stammered, clutching onto the string.

"Hang on, Piglet," cried Pooh from down below.

It wasn't long before Piglet was flying over Kanga's house. Kanga had just hopped outside to get the mail.

"Look, Mama," said Roo, peering out of his mother's pouch. "A kite!"

"That's not a kite," said Kanga. "It's Piglet!"

And before Kanga could say another word, Pooh skidded to a stop in front of her. "Happy Windsday, Kanga," he said. "Happy Windsday, Roo."

"Can I fly Piglet next, Pooh?" Roo asked.

But Pooh and Piglet had already breezed past little Roo.

"Oh dear, oh dear, oh-dear-oh-dear-oh-dear," cried Piglet as he swooped right and left in the gusty air.

"Oh bo-bo-bother," Pooh exclaimed, bouncing and sliding along below him.

When Piglet finally found the nerve to look down, there was Eeyore, looking up at him. Eeyore was busy repairing his house, which the wind had blown to pieces. He had just put the last stick back in place when Pooh came crashing through.

"Happy Windsday, Eeyore," said Pooh. Then he went zipping off again, still holding on to the remains of Piglet's scarf.

"Thanks for noticin' me," said Eeyore.

Not far from Eeyore's house was Rabbit's garden.

"Ah, what a refreshing day for harvesting," Rabbit said aloud as he pulled up a large orange carrot.

Looking up, he suddenly saw Pooh coming toward him at top speed.

"Oh no!" shouted Rabbit, waving his arms frantically.

"Happy Windsday," Pooh called, kicking up a whole row of carrots.

"Oh, *yes!*" Rabbit chuckled as the juicy, ripe carrots fell smack into his wheelbarrow.

Stronger and stronger the West Wind blew. And before long, Piglet found himself blown right up against Owl's window.

Owl was awakened from a peaceful snooze by the loud crash. "Whoo?" he said, opening his big round eyes. "Who is it?"

"It's me," Piglet said. "P-p-p-please, may I come in?"

"Well, I say now," Owl said, his eyes rounder than ever. "Someone has pasted Piglet on my window."

Just then Pooh's face appeared beside Piglet's, and Owl invited them both in. Soon Pooh and Piglet were comfortably seated in Owl's cozy living room. "Am I correct in assuming that it's a rather blustery day?" asked Owl.

"Oh, yes. That reminds me. Happy Windsday, Owl," said Pooh, hungrily eyeing a big honeypot in front of him on the table.

"Windsday?" Owl hooted as the wind whistled through his house. "My good fellow, I wouldn't go so far as to call it Windsday. Just a mild zephyr."

"Excuse me, Owl, but is there any honey in that pot?" Pooh shouted over the howling wind.

"Oh, yes, of course," Owl said. "Help yourself." While Pooh eagerly reached for the pot of honey—which the wind had just blown clear across the table—Owl continued with his story.

"As I was saying, this is just a mild zephyr compared to the big wind of sixty-seven. Or was it seventy-six?" Owl muttered, scratching his head. "Oh well, no matter. I remember the big blow well. It was the year my aunt Clara went to visit her cousin. Now, her cousin was not only gifted on the glockenspiel, but . . . "

And with the wild wind roaring through his house, Owl
proceeded to tell his friends all about his aunt Clara's cousin. He
didn't seem to notice when the teacups clattered to the floor. And
he barely paused when the wind swept Piglet right out the door
and back in again. It wasn't until the whole house came crashing
down upon his ears that Owl finally finished his tale.

As soon as Christopher Robin heard the news, he hurried to the scene of Owl's disaster.

"What a pity," said Christopher Robin when he saw the state Owl's house was in. "I don't think we will ever be able to fix it."

"If you ask me," said Eeyore, "when a house looks like that, it's time to find another one." Then he shook his head and said, "It might take a day or two, but don't worry, Owl—I'll find you a new one."

"Good," said Owl, settling back in his rocking chair. "That will just give me time to tell you about my uncle Clyde. . . ."

And that's just what he did. On and on Owl talked until the blustery day turned into a blustery night.

For Pooh it turned out to be an anxious sort of night, filled with anxious sorts of noises. One was a particular noise he'd never heard before:

"*Rrrrrr!*"

It wasn't a rumble. It wasn't a grumble. And it wasn't exactly a growl. But whatever it was, it was coming from just outside Pooh's door.

"Is that you, Piglet?" Pooh called, but no one answered. "Eeyore?" Pooh tried again. And finally, "Christopher Robin?"

When there was still no answer, Pooh got out of bed and went to investigate. And being a bear of very little brain, he decided to invite the new sound in.

"Hello?" he said, flinging the front door open.

Suddenly a big, bouncy creature bounded in and knocked Pooh flat on his back.

"*Rrrrrr.* Hello," the creature said from atop Pooh's chest. "I'm Tigger."

"Oh," Pooh replied, looking up into Tigger's smiling face. "You scared me."

"Sure I did," Tigger said good-naturedly. "Everyone's scared of Tiggers. Who are you?"

"I'm Pooh," said Pooh.

"Ah, what's a Pooh?" Tigger asked.

"You're sitting on one," Pooh informed him.

And with no further ado, Tigger climbed off Pooh, stuck out his paw, and said, "Glad to meet ya. Tigger's my name. T-I–double Guh–Er. That spells Tigger!"

"But what's a Tigger?" Pooh asked, plainly puzzled.

Without a pause, Tigger proudly replied:

The wonderful thing about Tiggers
is Tiggers are wonderful things.
Their tops are made out of rubber,
and their bottoms are made of springs.
They're bouncy, trouncy, flouncy, pouncy,
fun, fun, fun, fun, fun.
But the most wonderful thing about Tiggers
is that I'm the only one!

And to prove his point, Tigger bounced around the room on his springy tail repeating: "I'm the only one!"

"If you're the only one, what's that over there?" Pooh asked, pointing at Tigger's reflection in the mirror.

"What a strange-looking creature!" said Tigger. "Look at the beady little eyes, pur-posti-rus chin, and ricky-diculus striped pajamas!"

Pooh nodded, and then he said, "Looks like another Tigger to me."

Tigger decided to change the subject. "Ah, well, did I say I was hungry?"

"I don't think so," said Pooh.

"Well, then, I'll say it," said Tigger. "I'm hungry."

"Not for honey, I hope," Pooh said, casting a worried glance at his honeypot.

"Oh boy, honey!" Tigger cried. "That's what Tiggers like best."

"I was afraid of that," Pooh said as Tigger plopped down at the table, grabbed the honey, and dug his paw in.

"*Yum,*" Tigger said, putting a glob of honey in his mouth. "*Yuck!*" he said when he swallowed his first mouthful.

"Tiggers *don't* like honey," he gagged. "That sticky stuff is only fit for heffalumps and woozles."

"You mean elephants and weasels," Pooh corrected him.

"That's what I said. Heffalumps and woozles," Tigger said.

"Well, what do heff . . . ah . . . ah . . . hallalaff, ah . . . what do they do?" Pooh inquired.

"Oh, nothin' much," Tigger said nonchalantly. "Just steal honey." And with that, he went bouncing out the door and into the night.

Suddenly Pooh was all alone . . . Or was he?

Pooh had a horrible feeling that at least one heffalump—or was it a woozle?—was lurking about outside. So he bolted the door and picked up his pop gun, determined to stand guard over his honey.

Hour after hour, Pooh kept his lonely vigil while the very blustery night turned into a very rainy night. Lightning flashed. Thunder crashed. And somewhere between the flashing and crashing, Pooh fell asleep.

Pooh dreamed he was surrounded by heffalumps and woozles of all shapes and sizes. Some were black, and some were brown. Some were up, and some were down. Some had polka dots. Some had stripes. But they all had one thing in common: *they all wanted to steal his honey!*

As Pooh tightly clutched his honeypot, one of the heffalumps turned into a watering can and began dousing him with water. The chilly drops cascaded over Pooh, soaking him from head to toe.

He woke up suddenly, and the heffalumps and woozles were gone. But the water remained. It was already up to Pooh's knees, and more was leaking in through the ceiling.

Pooh slogged across the flooded floor to his mirror. After studying the very damp bear reflected there, he asked, "Is it raining where you are?" And without even waiting for an answer, he said, "It's raining where I am, too."

As a matter of fact, it was raining all over the Hundred-Acre Wood. The rain came down, down, down, and the river rose up, up, up, rising so high it finally crept out of its bed and into Piglet's.

Poor Piglet was terrified. With the water swirling around him, he grabbed paper and pen and frantically scribbled: HELP! P . . . P . . . PIGLET. (ME.) Then he placed the message in a bottle and tossed it out his window and into the raging river.

As the rain came down, Piglet tried to scoop it up into a big iron pot. But the pot was not—most definitely not!—big enough for all that water.

Floating atop a wooden chair, Piglet kept on bailing, but as he was bailing, he went sailing through the door.

Meanwhile, Pooh was having quite a difficult time himself. He had managed to save ten honeypots, and he sat with them on the branch of a tree, high above the river. More than ready for his supper, he stuck his head into one of the pots. But as Pooh tried to sop up his supper, the river sopped up Pooh, for he fell off the branch and into the swirling water below. Upside down, with his head still stuck in the honeypot, Pooh was carried along with the current.

The Hundred-Acre Wood got floodier and floodier. But the water couldn't come all the way up to Christopher Robin's house, so that's where everyone gathered. Everyone except Piglet, Pooh, and Eeyore, that is.

In the midst of all the excitement, Eeyore stubbornly stuck to his task of finding a new home for Owl.

While Eeyore was off house-hunting, Roo made an important discovery. "Look!" he said. "I've found a bottle, and it's got something in it, too."

"It's a message," Christopher Robin declared. "It says: 'Help! P . . . P . . . Piglet. (Me.)'"

Turning to Owl, he said, "You must fly over to Piglet's house and tell him we'll make a rescue."

So Owl flew out over the flood, and soon he spotted two small objects below him.

One was little Piglet, caught in a whirlpool. And the other was Pooh, floating downstream, his head still stuck in the honeypot.

"Oh, Owl," Piglet said. "I don't mean to c-c-complain, but I'm so s-s-scared."

"Be brave, little Piglet," Owl advised. "Chin up and all that sort of thing."

"It's awfully hard to be b-b-brave when you're such a s-s-small animal," Piglet pointed out.

"Then to divert your small mind from your unfortunate predicament, I shall tell you an amusing anecdote," Owl offered. "It concerns a distant cousin of mine. . . ."

Owl had just begun his story when Piglet cried, "I beg your pardon, Owl, but I think we're coming to a flutterfall, a falatterfall, a very big w-waterfall!"

"Please," said Owl, holding up a warning wing. "No interruptions."

But Piglet was already being carried away by the current. A moment later he fell over the falls, with Pooh Bear close behind.

Head over heels the two friends tumbled down the rushing, gushing waterfall—down, down, down until they finally landed in a quiet pool far, far, far below.

"Oh, there you are, Pooh Bear," Owl said as Pooh popped up on Piglet's chair. "Now, to continue my story. . ."

Fortunately for Pooh, Owl didn't have time to finish his story, for they quickly floated to the river's edge, where Christopher Robin and the others were waiting.

"Pooh!" Christopher Robin cried, lifting him off the chair. "Thank goodness you're safe. But where is Piglet?"

All of a sudden something emerged from under the chair. It was Pooh's honeypot!

"H-h-here I am," Piglet replied from inside the pot.

"Pooh!" Christopher Robin cried again. "You rescued Piglet."

"I did?" Pooh said.

"Yes," Christopher Robin said, patting Pooh on the head. "And it was a very brave thing to do. You are a hero!"

"I am?" Pooh said.

"Yes," Christopher Robin said. "And as soon as the flood is over, I shall give you a hero party."

Pooh's hero party had barely begun when Eeyore came trudging in.

"I found a house for Owl," he said.

"I say, Eeyore, good show!" Owl hooted happily. "Where, may I ask, is it?"

"Follow me, and I'll show you," Eeyore said.

So everyone followed Eeyore. But much to their surprise, when they got to Owl's new house, it turned out to be . . .

. . . Piglet's house!

"Why are we stopping here?" Christopher Robin asked.

"This is Owl's new house," Eeyore said proudly. "What do you think of it?"

There was a long moment of silence. Then Christopher Robin said, "It's a nice house, Eeyore, but . . ."

And Kanga said, "It's a lovely house, but . . ."

"It's the best house in the whole world," Piglet sighed, his eyes full of tears.

"Tell them it's your house, Piglet," Pooh whispered.

But Piglet didn't have the heart to disappoint Owl. "No," he said. "This house belongs—*sniff*—to our good friend Owl."

"But Piglet," Rabbit said, "where will *you* live?"

"Well . . . ," Piglet said. "I-I-I guess—*sniff*—I shall l-live . . . "

"With me," Pooh broke in, taking Piglet's hand in his. "You shall live with me, won't you, Piglet?"

"With you?" Piglet said, wiping a tear from his eye. "Oh, thank you, Pooh Bear. Of course I will."

"Piglet, that was a very grand thing to do," Christopher Robin said, taking Piglet's other hand.

"A heroic thing," Rabbit chimed in.

And that's when Pooh had his second good thought in two days. "Christopher Robin," he asked, "can we make a one-hero party into a two-hero party?"

"Of course we can, silly old bear," said Christopher Robin.

And so they did.

Pooh was a hero for saving Piglet, and Piglet was a hero for giving Owl his grand home in the beech tree.

To celebrate these deeds of bravery and generosity, everyone gathered round the heroes, shouting, "Hip, hip, hooray for the Piglet and the Pooh."

Then Pooh and Piglet were scooped up in a blanket and tossed high, high, high into the clear blue sky.

Walt Disney's

Winnie the Pooh and Tigger Too

Stephanie Calmenson

Illustrated by Ennis McNulty and Lou Paleno

One fine day in the Hundred-Acre Wood, Winnie the Pooh
was sitting on a comfortable log in his Thoughtful Spot when his
thoughts were interrupted by a sound he knew very well: *BOING!
BOING! BOING!*

"Hello, Pooh! It's me, Tigger!" exclaimed Tigger, bounding into
the Thoughtful Spot and bouncing Pooh right off his log. "T-
I–double Guh–Er spells Tigger!"

"Yes, I know," said Pooh. "You've bounced me before."

Tigger jumped up and shook Pooh's hand. "Well, I'd better be
going now. I have a lot more bouncing to do."

Nearby, Piglet was busy sweeping up outside his house. He began to hear a noise, which started off smaller than Piglet himself but quickly grew larger and larger. Suddenly the noise turned into Tigger, who bounced Piglet right off his feet.

"Ooh, Tigger. You scared me!" said Piglet.

"I did? But I gave you one of my littlest bounces. I'm saving my biggest one for old long ears," Tigger said. He pulled up his ears as far as they would go, trying to look like Rabbit.

"Well, I'm glad I got one of your little bounces. Thank you, Tigger," said Piglet. He waved good-bye as Tigger bounced off down the road in the direction of Rabbit's house.

"There, that should do it," said Rabbit as he gathered up an armload of carrots from his garden. But then he heard a sound he knew all too well: *BOING! BOING! BOING!*

"Oh no!" cried Rabbit. "Stop!"

But Tigger didn't stop. He bounced Rabbit right off his feet, sending the carrots flying every which way.

"Hello, Rabbit! It's me, Tigger," said Tigger. "That's T-I–double Guh–Er . . ."

"Oh, please, please! Don't spell it," moaned Rabbit, sitting up and pushing Tigger away. "Oh Tigger, won't you ever stop bouncing?"

"Why would I? Bouncing is what Tiggers do best. Hoo-hoo-*hoo!*" exclaimed Tigger. He started to sing:

Oh, the wonderful thing about Tiggers
is Tiggers are wonderful things.
Their tops are made out of rubber,
and their bottoms are made of springs.
They're bouncy, trouncy, flouncy, pouncy,
fun, fun, fun, fun, fun.
But the most wonderful thing about Tiggers
is that I'm the only one!

As Tigger bounced away, Rabbit stomped angrily around his garden, gathering up his scattered carrots. "Something must be done about that Tigger!" he said to himself.

That afternoon Rabbit invited Pooh and Piglet to a meeting at his house.

"I say, Tigger is getting too bouncy these days," Rabbit began. "Now, I've got a splendid idea. We'll take Tigger on an expedition to someplace he's never been. And then we'll lose him!"

"Lose him?" Pooh repeated. Losing someone didn't sound to him like a very friendly thing to do.

"Oh, we'll find him again the next morning," said Rabbit. "But by then he'll be a humble Tigger. A small and sad Tigger. An oh-Rabbit-am-I-glad-to-see-you Tigger. It will take those bounces right out of him." He rubbed his hands together eagerly.

The next morning crept into the Hundred-Acre Wood in a cold and misty sort of way. As Rabbit, Piglet, Pooh, and Tigger set off on their expedition, the mist was so thick that they could hardly see their feet at the ends of their legs.

Tigger bounced in circles around the others. He bounced ahead and came back again. Finally, he bounced off into some especially thick mist beside the trail, where he seemed to disappear.

"Quick," Rabbit said eagerly. "Now's our chance to lose him."

He ran into a hollow log and pulled Pooh and Piglet in behind him. Then he peeked out from inside the log and breathed a sigh of relief. Tigger was nowhere in sight.

"My splendid idea worked perfectly," Rabbit said with a chuckle. "Now we can all go home."

Pooh was very glad to hear that they were going home. "Yum, yum, time for lunch," he said.

"Halloo!" called a voice from not very far away.

"Oh no! It's you-know-who!" cried Rabbit. Before Pooh quite knew what was happening, Rabbit had grabbed him and pulled him back inside the log.

A second later Tigger bounced onto the very log where Rabbit, Piglet, and Pooh were hiding. "Halloo!" he shouted to the right. "Halloo!" he shouted to the left. Then he leaned down and shouted "Halloo!" right into the log.

Rabbit, Piglet, and Pooh shook all over as Tigger's shout echoed inside. But they didn't say a word.

Tigger hopped off the log and bounced away into the Hundred-Acre Wood, still calling, "Halloo!"

Rabbit jumped out of the log. "Hooray!" he cried. "We've done it! We've lost Tigger! We can go home now."

So they started off toward home.

"It's funny how everything looks the same in the mist," said Rabbit a few minutes later. "Take this sand pit, for instance. I'm sure we've seen it before."

"I'm sure you're right," said Pooh agreeably.

They kept walking, and in a little while they came upon the very same sand pit.

"Er . . . Rabbit? How would it be if as soon as we're out of sight of this old pit we try to find it again?" suggested Pooh. "Because, you see, we keep looking for home. But we keep finding this pit. So perhaps if we looked for this pit, we might find home."

"I don't see much sense in that," said Rabbit. "If I walked away from this pit and then walked back to it, of course I would find it again. Wait right here and I'll prove it to you."

With great determination, Rabbit set off into the mist. Pooh and Piglet sat down in the sand pit to wait for him to return.

They waited . . . and waited . . . and waited. Piglet fell fast asleep, leaning against Pooh's tummy. Suddenly he was awakened by a grumbling noise.

"What was that?" asked Piglet, jumping up.

"Why, I believe that was my tummy rumbling," said Pooh. "I'm awfully hungry. I think we should go home and have lunch."

"Do you know the way, Pooh?" asked Piglet.

"Well, I have twelve pots of honey in my cupboard that my tummy very much wants to find. So we can simply follow my tummy home," Pooh explained.

Piglet tried to be as quiet as possible so that Pooh's tummy could concentrate. Then, just as Piglet began to know where he was—

BOING! BOING! BOING!

It was Tigger! He bounced into Pooh and Piglet, rolling them over and over.

"Hello, there, you two!" he said. "Where have you been?"

"We've been trying to find our way back home," said Pooh.

"But we seem to have lost Rabbit somewhere in the mist," added Piglet.

"Leave it to me," said Tigger. "I'll bounce him out of there in no time!"

At that very moment Rabbit was just about as lost as a Rabbit could be. He was so scared that he was trembling from the tops of his ears all the way down to the tips of his toes. Little noises that he wouldn't even have noticed on a sunny day suddenly sounded loud and frightening. Soon Rabbit was so scared that he couldn't stand it anymore. He ran away as fast as his legs would carry him.

He wasn't looking where he was going and ran straight into . . .

"Tigger!" cried Rabbit. "You're supposed to be lost!" Rabbit couldn't remember ever being so happy to see Tigger before.

"Lost? Tiggers never get lost," said Tigger. "Come on, Rabbit. Let's go home. Hang on."

Tigger placed his tail in Rabbit's hand, then bounced off toward home. Rabbit held on tight as he was carried along through the mist and the mud. He was now a thoroughly humiliated Rabbit. A lost-and-found Rabbit. A why-oh-why-do-these-things-happen-to-me Rabbit.

But more than anything else, he was a happy-to-be-going-home Rabbit.

A short while after Rabbit's getting-lost adventure, it began to snow in the Hundred-Acre Wood. The snow fell quietly all night long. In the morning a soft white blanket covered all the houses in the forest, including the house where Kanga and baby Roo lived.

"Mama, when is Tigger going to get here?" asked Roo.

"Be patient, dear," said Kanga as she swept a path through the snow. "He'll be here soon."

Almost before the words were out of her mouth, Kanga and
Roo heard a familiar sound:

BOING! BOING! BOING!

Tigger slid into the yard, creating a wave of snow that knocked
Roo right off the mailbox.

"Here I am!" said Tigger. "Did I surprise you?"

"You sure did!" said Roo. "I like surprises. I like bouncing, too."

"I know," said Tigger. "That's why I'm here. I've come to take you bouncing with me."

"Hooray!" said Roo. "I'm all ready."

Roo and Tigger said good-bye to Kanga, and then Tigger led
the way out of the yard with his great big bounces:

BOING! BOING! BOING!

And Roo followed right behind with his very little ones:

BOING! BOING! BOING!

When Tigger and Roo had gone a short distance into the forest, Tigger called, "Hey, look, Roo. It's old long ears."

Sure enough, Roo spotted Rabbit up ahead, gliding happily across a frozen pond. In fact, Rabbit was enjoying his skating so much that he didn't even see Tigger and Roo.

"Can Tiggers ice-skate?" asked Roo. "As fancy as Mr. Rabbit can?"

"Oh-ho-ho!" said Tigger. "Ice-skating is what Tiggers do best. Watch!"

Tigger bounced onto the pond. "Whee! This is easy," he said as he slid across the ice. First he skated on one foot, then the other. Next he tried to skate on the tip of his tail. That's when he started wiggling . . .

and wobbling . . .

and sliding faster and faster across the ice—straight toward Rabbit.

"Look out!" Tigger cried. "I can't stop!"

When Rabbit turned and saw Tigger heading his way, his eyes grew very wide. He threw up his hands. "No! No! Don't!" he shouted.

But Tigger, who had very little choice in the matter, just kept on coming. He crashed right into Rabbit, then slid into the snow. Rabbit went flying through the front door of his house, knocking over everything inside.

"Why does it always have to be me?" moaned Rabbit. "Why, oh why, oh why?"

"*Yech,*" Tigger said, spitting out a mouthful of snow. "Tiggers do *not* like ice-skating."

Tigger and Roo left Rabbit and bounced farther into the Hundred-Acre Wood. "I bet you're good at climbing trees, huh, Tigger?" asked Roo.

"Hoo-hoo-*hoo!*" laughed Tigger. "That's what Tiggers do best. Only Tiggers don't climb trees, they bounce them. Come on, I'll show you!"

With Roo sitting on his shoulders, Tigger bounced from branch to branch to branch up to the very tippity-top of the very tallest tree he could find.

"Pretty good bouncing, huh?" said Tigger, looking down.

But when he saw how far he was from the ground, he wrapped his arms around the tree trunk and closed his eyes tight.

"Wait just a minute! How did this tree get so high?" said Tigger.

Suddenly he felt a tug on the end of his tail and looked down to see Roo swinging back and forth from the end of it.

"S-s-stop that, kid, please," begged Tigger. "You're rocking the forest!"

While Tigger was busy getting stuck in the tree, Pooh and Piglet were busy tracking some footprints around a bush. They stopped when they heard a loud "Hallooooo!"

"L-look, Piglet," said Pooh. "There's something in that tree over there."

"Hallooooo!" called the voice again.

"Pooh! Piglet!" called a second, smaller voice.

When he looked more carefully, Pooh saw that the something in the tree was Tigger and Roo. "Hello," said Pooh. "What are you two doing up there?"

"Well, I'm all right," said Roo. "But Tigger's stuck."

"Help! Somebody! Please, help!" cried Tigger. "Get Christopher Robin!"

It wasn't long before Christopher Robin arrived, with Kanga and Rabbit right behind him.

"My goodness," said Kanga, looking up. "How did you get way up there, Roo?"

"It was easy, Mama. We bounced up," said Roo. "But now Tigger's stuck."

"That's too bad," said Kanga.

"No, that's good," said Rabbit happily. "Tigger can't bounce anybody as long as he's stuck up in that tree."

"We can't just leave him up there. We have to get them both down," said Christopher Robin firmly. "Now, everybody take hold of my coat. Ready? Okay, you're first, Roo. Jump!"

"Try not to fall too fast, dear," Kanga said.

"Here I come. *Whee!*" cried Roo. He landed safely in the middle of Christopher Robin's coat, then popped up into Kanga's arms.

"That was fun!" said Roo. "Come on Tigger. Jump!"

"Jump? Tiggers don't jump. They bounce," said Tigger, clutching the tree tighter than ever.

"Then why don't you bounce down," suggested Pooh.

"Don't be ridiculous. Tiggers only bounce *up*," said Tigger.

"Then you'll have to climb down," said Christopher Robin.

"Tiggers can't climb down because . . . because their tails get in the way," said Tigger. And he wrapped his tail tightly around the tree branch.

"That settles it," said Rabbit. "If Tigger won't jump down or climb down, we'll just have to leave him up there forever!"

"Forever?" moaned Tigger. "Oh, if I ever get down from this tree, I promise never to bounce again."

"I heard that!" cried Rabbit, jumping for joy. "Did you all hear that? Tigger promised never to bounce again!"

"All right, Tigger," Christopher Robin called up to him. "It's time for you to come down now."

Finally Tigger unwound his tail from the branch and slo-o-o-owly and carefully climbed down.

As soon as his feet touched the ground, Tigger was his old cheerful self again. "Hey, I'm so happy to be out of that tree, I feel like bouncing!" he cried.

"No, no, no!" Rabbit said quickly. "You promised. No more bouncing."

"Uh-oh. I did promise, didn't I?" said Tigger. "Does that really mean I can never ever bounce again? Not even one teensy-weensy bounce?"

"Not a smidgen of a bounce," said Rabbit.

Tigger's tail flopped. His shoulders dropped. He walked off sadly towards home.

Tigger's friends watched him go. Rabbit was the only one with a smile on his face.

Roo tugged on Christopher Robin's coat. "Christopher Robin," he said. "I like the old bouncy Tigger best."

"So do I, Roo," said Christopher Robin.

"Me, too," said Piglet, and Pooh nodded.

"We all do," said Kanga. "Don't you agree, Rabbit?"

"Well," said Rabbit. "I . . . ah . . ." He thought about all the times Tigger had bounced him off his feet.

"Yes, Rabbit?" said Pooh.

"Well, you see," said Rabbit. "I . . . ah . . ." He thought about how sad Tigger had looked walking off without his bounce.

"Oh, all right," said Rabbit at last. "I guess I like the old Tigger better, too."

"Oh, boy!" shouted Tigger, who had heard Rabbit from far away. He returned with a quick bounce and knocked Rabbit off his feet. "You mean I can have my bounce back?" He picked up Rabbit and hugged him. "Come on, Rabbit. Let's bounce together."

Rabbit couldn't believe his ears. "Me? Bounce?" he said.

"Well, sure," said Tigger. "Look, you've got the feet for it."

"I do?"

Everyone looked down at Rabbit's feet. No one had ever noticed before what good bouncing feet they were.

Rabbit tried a little bounce . . . then a bigger one . . . then a bigger one than that. Before long he was bouncing just like Tigger. A smile spread across Rabbit's face.

"Well, come on, everybody!" he said.

So Pooh, Piglet, Kanga, Roo, Tigger, Rabbit, and Christopher Robin happily bounced together all through the Hundred-Acre Wood.

Walt Disney's

Winnie the Pooh and a Day for Eeyore

Teddy Slater

Illustrated by Bill Langley and John Kurtz

At the edge of the Hundred-Acre Wood, a lovely old bridge crossed a peaceful little river. Now, this bridge was a favorite spot of Winnie the Pooh's, and he would often wander there, doing nothing in particular and thinking nothing in particular. But on one such wandering, something suddenly took Pooh's mind off of nothing. And that something was a big brown pinecone, which dropped—*PLOP!*—right on his head.

Pooh picked up the pinecone and gazed at it thoughtfully. As he walked along, he decided to make up a little poem. But while his head was occupied (he was trying to think of a word that rhymed with *cone*), his feet, left to their own devices, tripped over a tree root, and Pooh tumbled to the ground.

Pooh kept on tumbling until he came to a stop on the bridge, just as the pinecone went skittering over the edge and into the water below.

"Oh bother," said Pooh. "I suppose I shall have to find another one."

Now, Pooh had every intention of doing just that. But the river was slipping away so peacefully beneath him that his thoughts began to slip away with it.

"That's funny," Pooh said to himself as the pinecone drifted under the bridge and floated lazily downstream. "I dropped it on one side, and it came out on the other.

"Hmm . . . ," he murmured, also to himself. "I wonder if it would do that again."

So he collected a rather large and a rather small pinecone and tossed them over the far side of the bridge. Then he scurried to the other side and waited.

"I wonder which one will come out first," said Pooh.

Well, as it turned out, the big one came out first, and the little one came out last, which was just what Pooh had hoped. And that was the beginning of a game called Pooh Sticks, named for its inventor—Winnie the Pooh.

Now, you might think it should have been called Pooh *Cones*, but since it was easier to collect a handful of sticks than an armful of cones, Pooh made a slight improvement on his original game.

And so it came to pass that one fine day Pooh, Piglet, Rabbit, and Roo were all on the bridge playing Pooh Sticks.

"All right now," Rabbit said. "The first stick to pass all the way under the bridge wins. On your marks, get set, . . . go!"

Pooh, Piglet, Rabbit, and Roo all threw their sticks into the water. Then they raced to the other side of the bridge to see whose would come out first.

"I can see mine," Roo shouted, pointing to a short black stick in the water. "I win! I win!" he cried, even as the "stick" suddenly spread its wings and flew off to join the other dragonflies flitting about.

"Can you see yours, Pooh?" Piglet asked, peering down at the gently flowing river.

"No," Pooh said. "I expect my stick's stuck."

"They always take longer than you think," Rabbit assured him just as something long, gray, and quite sticklike floated into view.

"Oh, I can see yours, Piglet," Pooh cried.

"Are you sure it's mine?" Piglet asked doubtfully.

"Sure," said Roo, "it's a gray one. A very big gray one."

"Oh, no, it isn't," said Rabbit. "It's . . . it's . . ."

"Eeyore!" everyone shouted.

"Don't pay any attention to me," Eeyore muttered as he floated by his friends, tail first. "Nobody ever does."

Rabbit leaned over the bridge. "Eeyore," he cried. "What are you doing down there?"

"I'll give you three guesses," Eeyore said flatly.

"Fishing?" asked Pooh.

"Wrong," said Eeyore.

"Going for a sail?" Roo guessed.

"Wrong again!"

"Ah, waiting for somebody to help you out of the river?" Rabbit tried.

"That's right," Eeyore mumbled more or less to himself. "Give Rabbit the time and he'll get the answer."

Piglet looked down at his friend in alarm. "Eeyore," he cried, "what can we . . . I mean, how should we . . . do you think if we . . ."

"Yes," Eeyore said calmly, "one of those would be just the thing. Thank you, Piglet."

"I've got an idea," Pooh offered hesitantly. "But I don't suppose it's a very good one."

"I don't suppose it is," Eeyore gurgled as his head tipped beneath the water.

"Go on, Pooh," Rabbit urged. "Let's have it."

"Well," Pooh said, "if we all threw stones and things into the
river on one side of Eeyore, the stones would make waves, and the
waves would wash him to the other side."

"That's a fine idea," said Rabbit. "I'm glad we thought of it,
Pooh." But Pooh had already gone off to find a suitable stone.

Eeyore floated around and around in a circle until finally Pooh
reappeared, rolling a great big boulder onto the bridge.

Rabbit immediately took charge. "Piglet," he directed, "give Pooh a little more room. Roo, get back a bit." And to Pooh he said, "I think a little to the left. No, no, a little to the right."

It took a while, but Pooh finally got the stone lined up to Rabbit's satisfaction. "Pooh," Rabbit said then, "when I say 'Now,' you can drop it."

Then he turned to Eeyore and said, "When I say 'Now,' Pooh
will drop the stone. Are you ready . . . ?

"One . . . ," Rabbit counted. "Two . . . ," and, "now!" he cried.

And with that, Pooh gave a mighty heave that sent the boulder
off the bridge—and right smack on top of Eeyore!

"Oh dear," Pooh sighed as Eeyore sank out of sight. "Perhaps it
wasn't such a very good idea after all."

Pooh was still peering woefully at the spot where his friend had disappeared when Eeyore came sloshing out of the water and onto the riverbank.

"Oh, Eeyore," Piglet squealed. "You're all wet."

"That happens when you've been in a river a long time," Eeyore said, shaking himself dry and giving Piglet a bit of a bath in the process.

"How did you fall in the river, Eeyore?" Rabbit asked.

"I didn't *fall* in," Eeyore said. "I was *bounced* in! I was just sitting by the side of the river, minding my own business, when I received a loud bounce."

"But who did it?" Pooh wanted to know.

"I expect it was T-Tigger," Piglet replied.

The words were no sooner out of Piglet's mouth than Tigger himself bounced onto the scene and knocked Rabbit flat on his back!

"Eyore," Rabbit said, scrambling to his feet, "was it Tigger who bounced you?"

"I didn't bounce him," said Tigger. "I happened to be behind Eeyore and I . . . I simply coughed."

"You bounced me," Eeyore said accusingly.

"I didn't bounce," Tigger repeated. "I coughed."

"Bouncing or coughing," Eeyore said, "it's all the same."

"Oh no, it's not," Tigger insisted.

But after several more rounds of "Bounced!" "Coughed!" "Did not!" "Did too!" Tigger finally admitted that he had in fact bounced Eeyore into the water.

"It was just a joke," he said sheepishly. But no one was laughing, least of all Eeyore.

"Some people have no sense of humor," Tigger grumbled as he went bouncing off into the woods.

"Tigger is so thoughtless," Rabbit said.

"Why should Tigger think of me?" Eeyore said. "No one else does."

"Why do you say that, Eeyore?" Pooh asked, but Eeyore was already shambling away, head hung, shoulders drooping.

Eeyore followed the stream back to his Gloomy Spot. As he sat there under what seemed to be his very own rain cloud, he could see his sad face in the water. "Pathetic," Eeyore said to his reflection.

Eeyore lumbered around to the other side of the bank and peered into the water again. "Just as I thought," he said. "No better from here. Pa-thetic," he repeated.

At the sound of footsteps, Eeyore looked up. And there was his friend Pooh.

"Eeyore," Pooh said softly. "What's the matter?"

"What makes you think anything's the matter?" Eeyore sighed.

"You seem so sad," said Pooh.

"Why should I be sad?" Eeyore asked sadly. And then, answering his own question, he said, "It's my birthday. The happiest day of the year."

"Your birthday?" Pooh said, surprised.

"Of course," Eeyore said. "Can't you see the presents?"

"No," Pooh replied, looking around in confusion.

"Can't you see the cake?" Eeyore went on. "The candles and the pink icing?"

"Well, no," Pooh said, more confused than before.

"Neither can I," Eeyore said with a sigh.

"Oh," said Pooh. Not quite sure what to say next, he said, "Well, many happy returns of the day, Eeyore."

"Thank you, Pooh," Eeyore said. "But we can't all . . . And some of us don't."

"Can't all what?" Pooh asked.

"No gaiety," Eeyore intoned. "No song and dance. No 'Here We Go Round the Mulberry Bush.' But don't worry about me, Pooh," he said. "Go and enjoy yourself. I'll stay here and be miserable, with no presents, no cake, and no candles. . . ."

As Eeyore's mournful voice trailed off, Pooh gently patted him on the back and said, "Eeyore, wait right here." Then he hurried off as fast as he could.

When Pooh got home, he found Piglet jumping up and down at the door, trying desperately to reach the door knocker.

"Here, let me do it," said Pooh, lifting the knocker.

"B-but Pooh—," Piglet started.

"I found out what's troubling Eeyore," Pooh interrupted. "It's his birthday, and nobody has taken any notice of it."

Pooh looked at the still-closed door. "Well, whoever lives here certainly takes a long time to answer the door."

"But Pooh, isn't this . . . your house?" asked Piglet.

"Oh, so it is," answered Pooh.

As the two friends went inside, Pooh declared, "I must get poor Eeyore a present. But what?" he wondered, looking around for a likely gift.

Just then Pooh spied a small honeypot in the pantry. "Ah, honey," he cried. "That should do very well." And turning to Piglet, he said, "What are you giving Eeyore?"

For a moment poor Piglet seemed quite at a loss, but then he said, "Perhaps I could give Eeyore a balloon."

"That," said Pooh, "is a very good idea!"

"I have one at home," Piglet exclaimed. "I'll go and get it right now."

So off Piglet hurried in one direction, and off Pooh went in the other.

Pooh hadn't gone far when a funny feeling crept over him. It began at the very tip of his nose and trickled all the way down to his toes. It was as if someone inside him were saying, "Now then, Pooh, time for a little something."

So Pooh reached into the honeypot and had a little something. Then he had a little more, and still a little more. And before long he had licked the honeypot clean.

As Pooh absentmindedly wiped the last sticky drop from his mouth, he said, "Now, where was I going? Oh yes, Eeyore. I was . . ." And looking down at the empty jar he said, "Oh bother, I must give Eeyore something."

But first, Pooh decided, he'd go visit his good friend Owl.

Owl was busy hanging a picture of his great-uncle Robert on the wall when Pooh knocked at the door.

"Many happy returns of Eeyore's birthday," Pooh said.

"You know, that reminds me of a birthday of my great-uncle Robert," Owl said, waving Pooh in with one wing and pointing to the newly hung portrait with the other.

"Uncle Robert had just reached the ripe old age of one hundred and three," Owl explained, "though of course he would only admit to ninety-seven. We all felt that a celebration was in order, so . . ."

"What are you giving him?" Pooh broke in the moment Owl paused for breath.

"Giving who?" Owl asked, peering quizzically at Pooh.

"Eeyore," Pooh replied.

"Oh, Eeyore," Owl chuckled. "Of course! I, ah . . . Well, what are *you* giving him, Pooh?"

"I'm giving him this useful pot to keep things in," said Pooh, holding out the empty honeypot, "and I—"

"A useful pot?" said Owl, peering into the jar. "Evidently someone has been keeping honey in it."

"Yes," said Pooh. "It's very useful like that, but I wanted to ask you—"

"You ought to write 'Happy Birthday' on it," said Owl.

"That was what I wanted to ask you," explained Pooh. "My own spelling is a bit wobbly."

"Very well," Owl said. And he took the pot and his pen and got down to work. "It's easier if people don't look while I'm writing," he added, turning his back on Pooh.

After what seemed a rather long time, Owl turned around again. "There!" he said, proudly holding up the pot. "All finished. What do you think of it?"

"It looks like a lot of words just to say 'Happy Birthday,'" Pooh pointed out.

"Well, actually, I wrote 'A Very Happy Birthday, with Love from Pooh,'" Owl explained. "Naturally it takes a good deal of words to say something like that."

"Oh, I see," Pooh said, taking the pot. "Thank you, Owl."

While Pooh went to deliver his gift to Eeyore, Owl headed off to Christopher Robin's house. On the way, he flew directly over Piglet, who was running along with a big red balloon.

"Many happy returns of Eeyore's birthday, Piglet," Owl hollered down.

"Many happy returns to you, too, Owl," Piglet hollered up.

But as Piglet hollered up, he neglected to look down and ran smack into a tree.

Piglet bounced off the tree and came to a stop—*POP!*—right on top of what *had been* the big red balloon.

"Oh d-d-dear. How shall I . . . ? What shall I . . . ? Well . . . maybe Eeyore doesn't like balloons so very much," Piglet said.

So he trudged off to Eeyore's, dragging the remains of the balloon behind him. Piglet found his friend moping under a leafless tree.

"Many happy returns of the day," Piglet sang out.

"Meaning my birthday," Eeyore said glumly.

"Yes," said Piglet. "And I've brought you a present."

"Pardon me, Piglet," Eeyore said, perking up. "My hearing must be going. I thought you said you brought me a present."

"I did," said Piglet. "I brought you a b-balloon."

"Balloon?" Eeyore echoed, his ears pricking up. "Did you say 'balloon'?"

"Yes," Piglet said. "But I'm afraid, I'm very sorry, but when I was running, that is, to bring it, I . . . I . . ."

Piglet's words wound down as he held out what was left of Eeyore's birthday balloon.

Eeyore took one look and said, "Red. My favorite color. How big was it?" he couldn't help asking.

"About as big as m-me," Piglet replied.

"My favorite size," Eeyore said wistfully.

Eeyore was sadly eyeing the shredded red balloon when Pooh appeared. "I've brought you a little present, Eeyore," he announced. "It's a useful pot. It's got 'A Very Happy Birthday, with Love from Pooh' written on it. And it's for putting things in."

"Like a balloon?" Eeyore said hopefully.

"Oh, no. Balloons are much too big . . . ," Pooh began, even as Eeyore picked the balloon up with his teeth and dropped it into the very useful pot.

"It *does* fit!" Pooh marveled as Eeyore carefully pulled the
balloon out of the pot, then dropped it back in again.

"Eeyore, I'm very glad I thought of giving you a useful pot to
put things in," said Pooh.

"And I'm very glad I thought of giving you something to put in
a useful pot," said Piglet.

Eeyore didn't say anything. But he looked very, very glad.

It was then that Christopher Robin arrived, along with Owl, Kanga, Roo, Rabbit, and a lovely chocolate birthday cake!

After his friends all sang "Happy Birthday," Eeyore made a wish and blew out the candles. Then Owl clapped his wings and cried, "Bravo! Good show! This reminds me of the party we once gave for my great-uncle Robert. . . ."

Owl had barely begun his story when he was interrupted by a cheerful "Halloo!"

"Oh no! Oh no! Oh no!" cried Rabbit just as Tigger bounced right into him and knocked him to the ground.

"Hello, Tigger," said Roo. "We're having a party."

"A party!" cried Tigger. "Oh boy, oh boy, oh boy. Tiggers love parties." And with no further ado, he bounced over to the table and gobbled up a fistful of cake.

"You've got a lot of nerve showing up here after what you did to Eeyore," Rabbit scolded Tigger. "I think you should leave now."

"Aw, let him stay," cried Roo.

"What do you think, Christopher Robin?" Pooh asked.

"I think," said Christopher Robin, "we all ought to play Pooh Sticks."

And that's exactly what they did.

Eeyore, who had never played the game before, won more times than anybody else. But poor Tigger didn't win at all.

When it was time for everyone to go home, Tigger threw down his stick and grumbled, "Tiggers don't like Pooh Sticks!" Then, instead of going off in his usual bouncy way, he walked off with his head down and no bounce at all.

"I'd be happy to tell you my secret for winning at Pooh Sticks," Eeyore said, hurrying after Tigger. "It's easy. You just have to let your stick drop in a twitchy sort of way."

"Oh yeah," said Tigger, brightening up immediately. "I forgot to twitch. That was my problem." And then, just because he was feeling so happy, he began bouncing again.

And of course he bounced right into Eeyore.

Meanwhile, Pooh, Piglet, and Christopher Robin lingered on the bridge, quietly watching the peaceful stream.

At last Piglet said, "Tigger's all right, really."

"Of course he is," Christopher Robin agreed.

"Everybody is, really," Pooh mused. "That's what I think." He hesitated a moment, then added, "But I don't suppose I'm right."

"Of course you are," said Christopher Robin, patting Pooh's head. "Silly old bear."